For Fred^K. Duffell
M.W.

my
great
granpa

For Mum
D.M.

First published 1990 by Walker Books Ltd
87 Vauxhall Walk, London SE11 5HJ

This edition published 2001

2 4 6 8 10 9 7 5 3 1

Text © 1990 Martin Waddell
Illustrations © 1990 Dom Mansell

This book has been typeset in Garamond

Printed in Hong Kong

British Library Cataloguing in Publication Data:
a catalogue record for this book is
available from the British Library

ISBN 0-7445-7865-5

MY GREAT GRANDPA

Martin Waddell   illustrated by Dom Mansell

WALKER BOOKS
AND SUBSIDIARIES
LONDON • BOSTON • SYDNEY

My Great Grandpa is slow.
His eyes are weak and
his legs don't go.
But he knows things that
no one else knows,
things he tells me about
when we go out.

Sometimes we go when my
Gran doesn't know.
He calls me his bus driver.
I call him my baby.
He makes bussy noises and
I push his pram.
People stare,
but we don't care!

My Great Grandpa knows
all about our town,
who lived where and
when and how.
But he can't remember who
lives here *now*.
So I have to tell him.
He says I'm as smart as a button,
but a button isn't much.

Our favourite place is his old house at the
bend at the end of the lane.
We go there again and again and
again and again and again and again.
We call it our house.

My Great Grandpa says it was his house
when Gran was like me, his little mouse.
But I'm not a mouse,
I'm a LION!

He says my Great Granny had eyes like mine
and they'd shine.
Then he sits for a while and starts to smile
and I think it's nice
'cos he loves her
. . . still.

My Great Grandpa knows where the berries are,
but it's too far.
We don't go picking berries.
We get them in Ted's shop instead.
Great Grandpa says berries
are bad for his burps,
but he eats so many
you'd think he would burst,
almost as many as me.

My Great Grandpa says I'm his special girl,
like my Gran was when she was young,
and my Mum and then me.
He says we are peas from a pod.
I say I'm a runner bean!
And then he says, "Let's go to the swings."

My Great Grandpa doesn't swing or do *anything*.
He sits and he nods and he smiles.
And he thinks of the things that he knows
that no one else knows.
He calls himself "Crow on the Shelf".
He's the nicest old crow that I know,
and I tell him so.

The sun makes Great Grandpa hot and grumpy.

So we go home.

And he goes to bed to rest his old head.

And I sit with my Gran on the grass in the sun.
She says, "It's sad to be like
Great Grandpa is now!"

But I know it's NOT!
For my Great Grandpa knows things
that no one else knows.
In his mind he goes places
that no one else goes.
He's got me, he's got Gran
and my Mum,
and we love him a lot . . .

but he shouldn't go out
when it's hot!

MARTIN WADDELL says of *My Great Grandpa,* "Some children relate instinctively to older people, and enjoy being with them, but I hope this story will help children who find old age confusing or distressing to understand that the old and infirm have once been young."

Martin Waddell is one of the finest contemporary writers of books for young people. Twice winner of the Smarties Book Prize – for *Farmer Duck* and *Can't You Sleep, Little Bear?* – he also won the Kurt Maschler Award for *The Park in the Dark* and the Best Books for Babies Award for *Rosie's Babies.* Among his many other titles are *Owl Babies; The Toymaker; Night Night, Cuddly Bear* and *A Kitten Called Moonlight.* He was the Irish nominee for the 2000 Hans Christian Andersen Award.

DOM MANSELL says, "I dedicated this book to my mum. Her dad lost both his legs as a result of the First World War, and I used to imagine her pushing Grandad around in his wheelchair. So, for me, the book is like a little tribute to my grandfather, Archie Backhouse."

As a child, Dom Mansell supplemented his pocket money by having his pictures of monsters printed in comics. In his adult life, he continues to be gainfully employed as an illustrator. His first book, Oscar Wilde's *The Selfish Giant,* was the runner-up for the Mother Goose Award, and has been followed by several others, including *Judy the Bad Fairy, Terrormazia* and *Mousemazia.* He lives in Sheffield.

ISBN 0-7445-3660-X (pb)

ISBN 0-7445-2335-4 (pb)

ISBN 0-7445-7294-0 (pb)

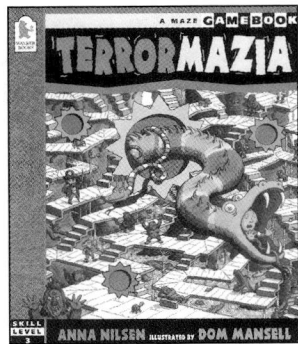

ISBN 0-7445-4708-3 (pb)

Owen

· KEVIN HENKES ·

SCHOLASTIC INC.

New York Toronto London Auckland Sydney
Mexico City New Delhi Hong Kong Buenos Aires

FOR LAURA

ISBN 0-439-68618-0

12 11 10 9 8 7 6 5 4 3 2 1   5 6 7 8 9/0

Printed in the U.S.A.   40

First Scholastic printing, September 2004

Watercolor paints and a black pen were used for the full-color art. The text type is Goudy Modern.

Owen had a fuzzy yellow blanket.

He'd had it since he was a baby.

He loved it with all his heart.

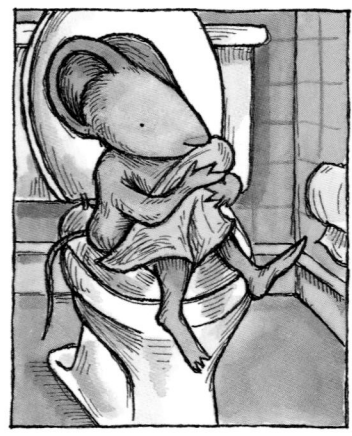  

"Fuzzy goes where I go," said Owen.

And Fuzzy did.

Upstairs, downstairs, in-between.

Inside, outside, upside down.

"Fuzzy likes what I like," said Owen.

And Fuzzy did.

Orange juice, grape juice, chocolate milk.

Ice cream, peanut butter, applesauce cake.

"Isn't he getting a little old to be carrying that thing around?" asked Mrs. Tweezers. "Haven't you heard of the Blanket Fairy?"

Owen's parents hadn't.

Mrs. Tweezers filled them in.

That night Owen's parents told Owen to put Fuzzy under his pillow.

In the morning Fuzzy would be gone, but the Blanket Fairy would leave an absolutely wonderful, positively perfect, especially terrific big-boy gift in its place.

Owen stuffed Fuzzy inside his pajama pants
and went to sleep.

"No Blanket Fairy," said Owen in the morning.

"No kidding," said Owen's mother.

"No wonder," said Owen's father.

"Fuzzy's dirty," said Owen's mother.

"Fuzzy's torn and ratty," said Owen's father.

"No," said Owen. "Fuzzy is perfect."

And Fuzzy was.

Fuzzy played Captain Plunger with Owen.

Fuzzy helped Owen become invisible.

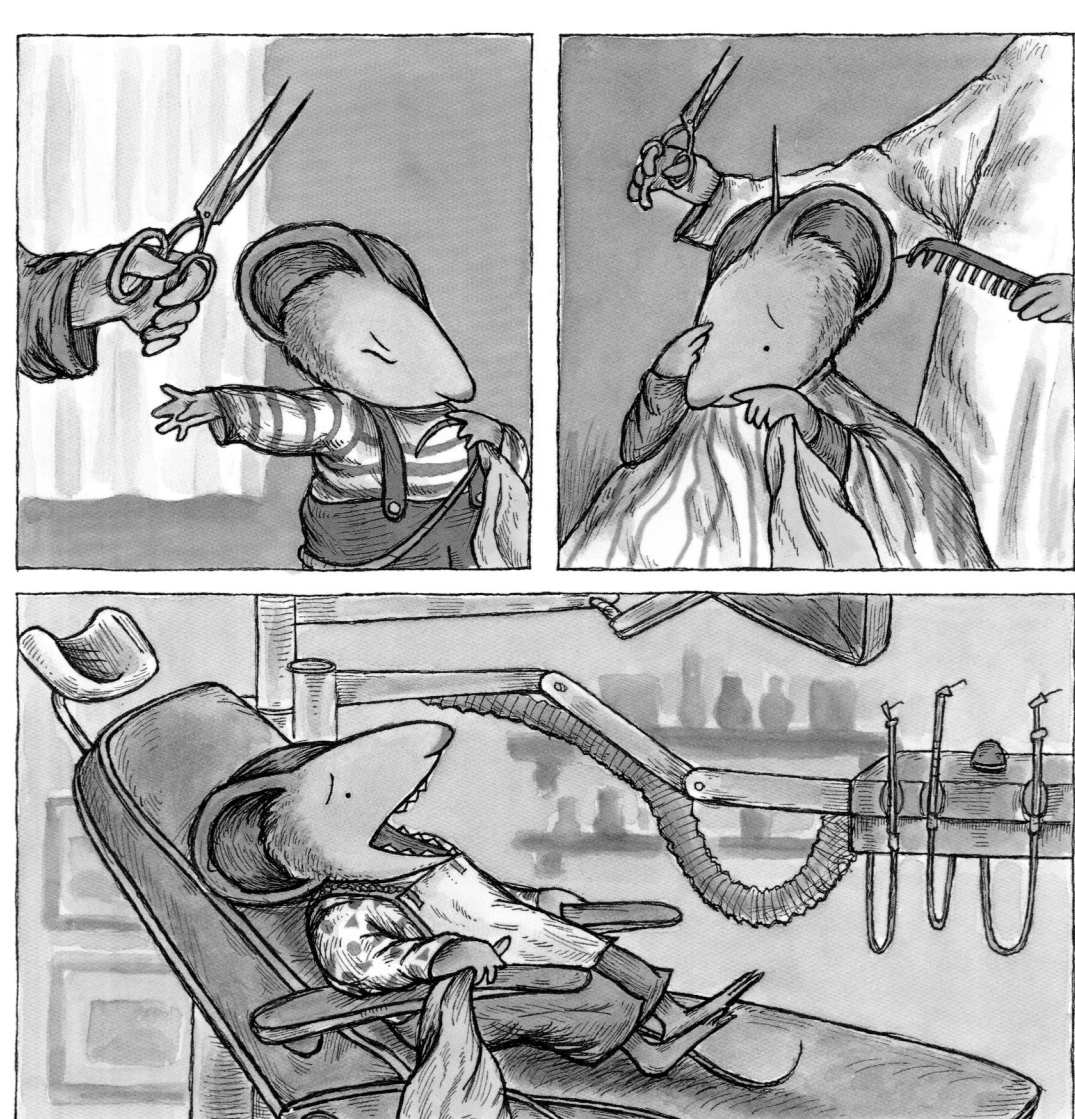

And Fuzzy was essential when it came to nail clippings
and haircuts and trips to the dentist.

"Can't be a baby forever," said Mrs. Tweezers.

"Haven't you heard of the vinegar trick?"

Owen's parents hadn't.

Mrs. Tweezers filled them in.

When Owen wasn't looking, his father dipped Owen's favorite corner of Fuzzy into a jar of vinegar.

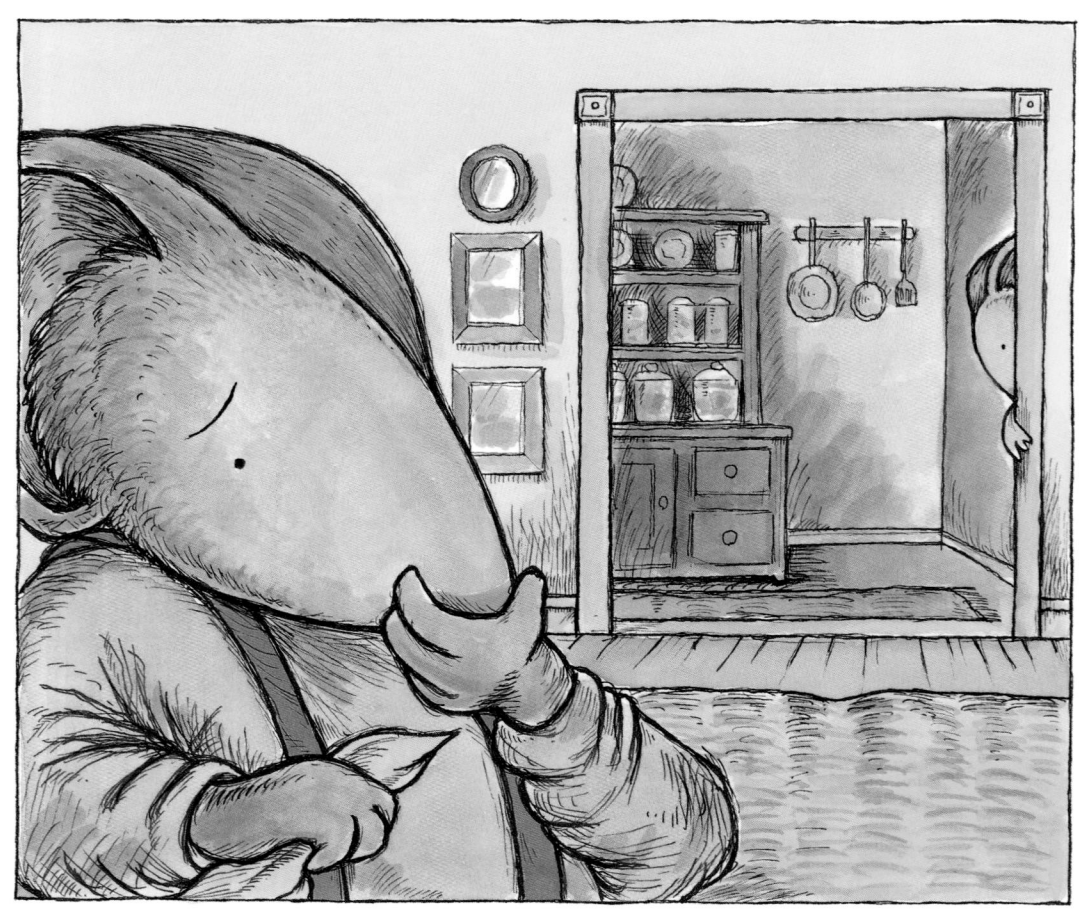

Owen sniffed it and smelled it and sniffed it.

He picked a new favorite corner.

Then he rubbed the smelly corner all around his sandbox,
buried it in the garden, and dug it up again.
"Good as new," said Owen.

Fuzzy wasn't very fuzzy anymore.

But Owen didn't mind.

He carried it.

And wore it.

And dragged it.

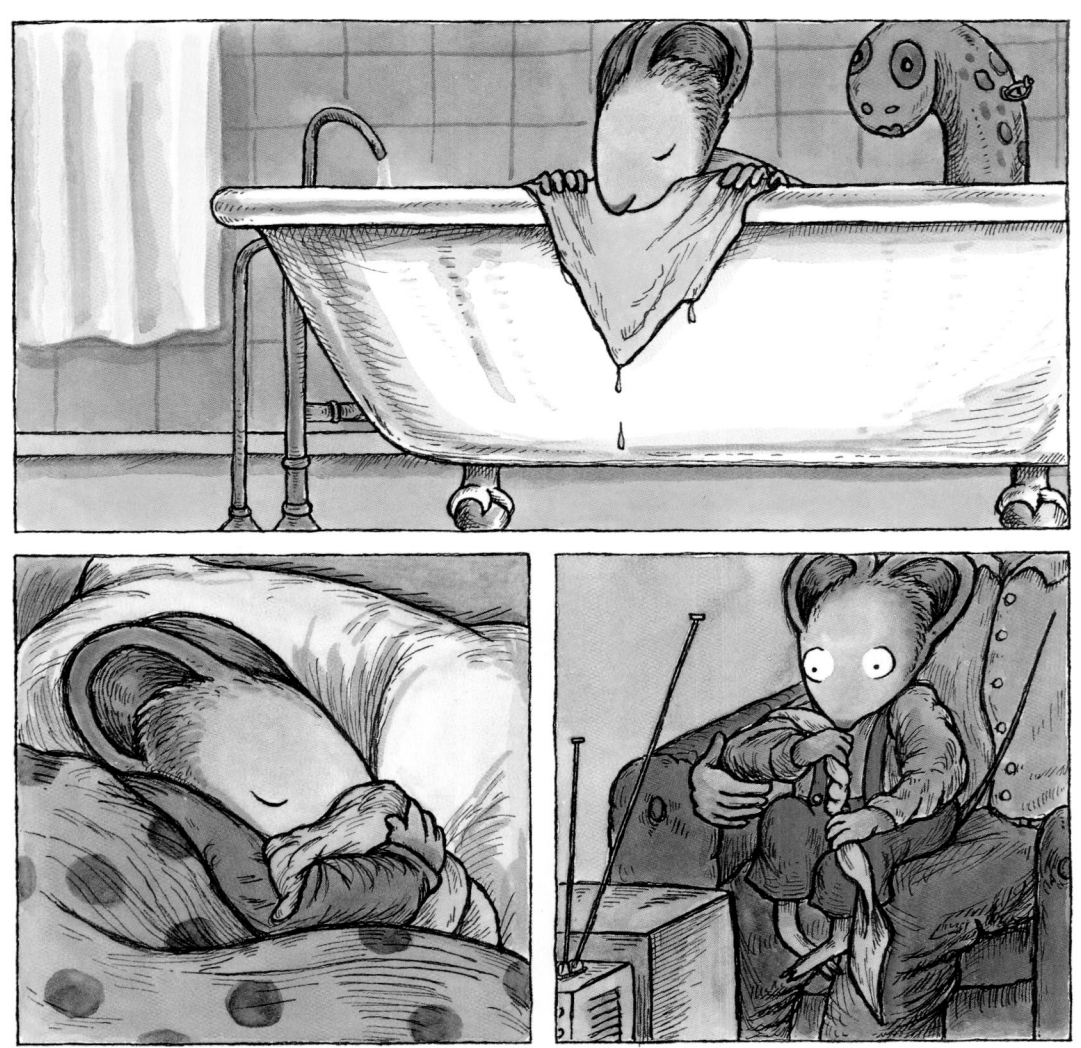

He sucked it.

And hugged it.

And twisted it.

"What are we going to do?" asked Owen's mother.

"School is starting soon," said Owen's father.

"Can't bring a blanket to school," said Mrs. Tweezers.

"Haven't you heard of saying no?"

Owen's parents hadn't.

Mrs. Tweezers filled them in.

"I *have* to bring Fuzzy to school," said Owen.

"No," said Owen's mother.

"No," said Owen's father.

Owen buried his face in Fuzzy.

He started to cry and would not stop.

"Don't worry," said Owen's mother.

"It'll be all right," said Owen's father.

And then suddenly Owen's mother said, "I have an idea!"

It was an absolutely wonderful, positively perfect, especially terrific idea.

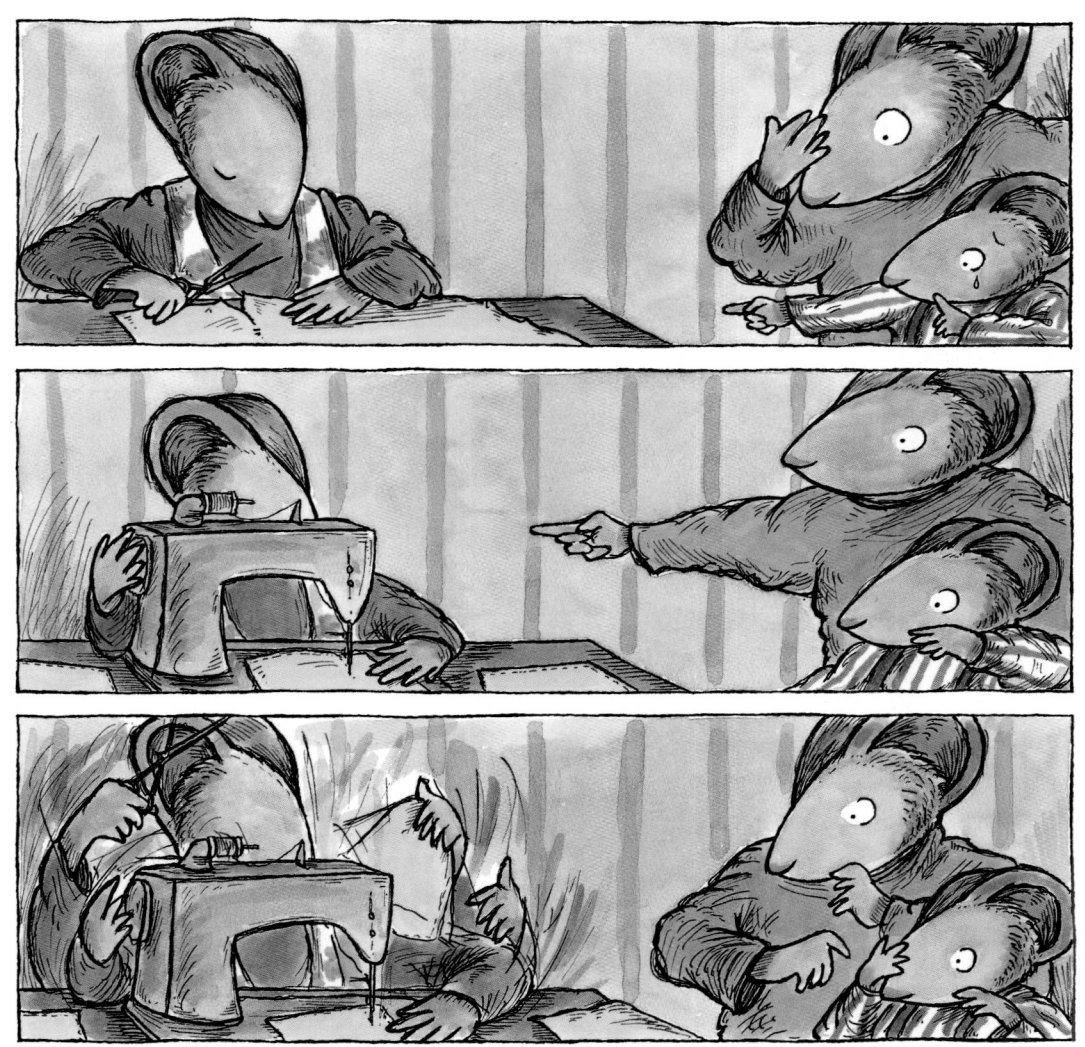

First she snipped.

And then she sewed.

Then she snipped again and sewed some more.

Snip, snip, snip.

Sew, sew, sew.

"Dry your eyes."

"Wipe your nose."

Hooray, hooray, hooray!

Now Owen carries one of his not-so-fuzzy handkerchiefs with him wherever he goes....

And Mrs. Tweezers doesn't say a thing.